To Neil and Margaret Meacher, for all their love
and support over the years – E.D.

A TEMPLAR BOOK

First published in the UK in 2009 by Templar Publishing,
an imprint of The Templar Company Limited,
The Granary, North Street, Dorking, Surrey, RH4 1DN, UK
www.templarco.co.uk

First edition

ISBN 978-1-84011-168-2

Designed by Mike Jolley
Edited by Libby Hamilton

Printed in China

Emma Dodd

Miaow
said the COW

templar publishing

Early one morning, Cat was sleeping, dreaming of hunting, stalking and leaping, when all of a sudden, out of the blue...

Cat thought for a while and came up with a trick,
for he loved casting spells and doing magic.

When the sun rose next morning, all pink and red,
Cockerel, as usual, threw back his head.
He puffed out his chest and opened his beak...

...and out came the tiniest,
"Squeak, squeak, squeak!"

"Ah-ha!" thought Cat,
with a sly little smirk.
"It seems that my spells
are beginning to work."

Pig woke next
and started yawning,
wanting his food,
as he did every morning.

He stretched his legs
and rolled in the muck,
then greedily grunted...

"Cluck!"

Out in the field was more mischief from Cat –
the sheep were all barking, running this way and that!
Sheepdog was muddled – it seemed so bizarre –
his "woof" had gone missing,
he could only say "Baa!"

The horse was quacking, the ducks were neighing –
nobody knew quite what they were saying!

Cat's clever plan had got out of hand.
The animals were louder than a big brass band!
So he crept away for a tasty snack –
a mouse or two from the old haystack.

By now the animals all could tell
that Cat was behind this beastly spell!
They were all feeling a little bit cross.
"It's time to show that cat who's boss!"

Suddenly, there was a deafening...

Moo!"

Cat was in trouble, that much he knew.

Then **all** of the animals, small and big –
the mice and hens, the clucking pig,
the sheep and ducks, dog, cow and horse,
and squeaking cockerel of course –

chased that cat

right through the barn,

across the yard,

out of the farm.

Squeak! **Miaow!**

Give us back OUR voices, now!"

What a noise they made
– a cacophony –
as they chased the cat
up the apple tree.

There really was
an awful din.
"OK," said Cat,
"you win, you win!
But you must admit,
it has been fun!"
With a flick of his tail,
the spells were undone.

All,
that is,
except
for
one...

Now every morning
it's Cat instead,
who opens his mouth
and throws back
his head...

"C

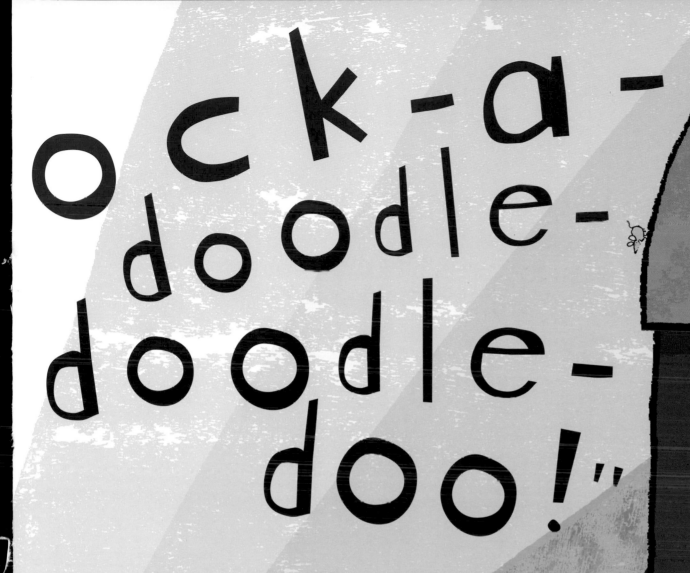

ock-a-
doodle-
doodle-
doodle-
doo!"

"Well," laugh the animals,
"that'll teach **you!**"